poochie-poo

Poochie-Poo

Helen Stephens

Picture Corgi Books

Thankyou to David (person), Maria (person), Ness (person) and Victor (pooch).

POOCHIE-POO
A PICTURE CORGI BOOK 9780552561761

First published in Great Britain by David Fickling Books,
a division of Random House Children's Books

David Fickling edition published 2002
Picture Corgi edition published 2003

3 5 7 9 10 8 6 4 2

Copyright © Helen Stephens, 2002

Picture Corgi Books are published by Random House Children's Books,
61–63 Uxbridge Road, London W5 5SA,
a division of The Random House Group Ltd,
in Australia by Random House Australia (Pty) Ltd,
20 Alfred Street, Milsons Point, Sydney, NSW 2061, Australia,
in New Zealand by Random House New Zealand Ltd,
18 Poland Road, Glenfield, Auckland 10, New Zealand,
and in South Africa by Random House (Pty) Ltd,
Endulini, 5A Jubilee Road, Parktown 2193, South Africa

THE RANDOM HOUSE GROUP Limited Reg. No. 954009
www.kidsatrandomhouse.co.uk

A CIP catalogue record for this book is available from the British Library.

Printed in Singapore

Victor is a well-behaved,
lovable pup and he lives
with *Miss Loopy.*

Miss Loopy adores **Victor**. She kisses him and cuddles him whenever she can. She buys him treats, and her favorite thing is to tickle him under his chin and say "Coo-chi-coo!" **Victor** loves being tickled and fussed over except . . .

. . . when his friend **Butch** comes to visit. **Butch** is a very small, very naughty pup. **Victor** thinks **Butch** is cool.

One day **Butch** came to visit.
"You two pups play nicely,"
said *Miss Loopy*.
"I'm not playing nicely," said
Butch. "Let's play baddies."
"Yes," said **Victor**. "Let's
play baddies."

"Here are some doggy biscuits,
you two pups," said *Miss Loopy.*
"Delicious!" said **Victor**.

"Baddies don't eat
doggy biscuits,"
said **Butch**.
"They eat table legs!"

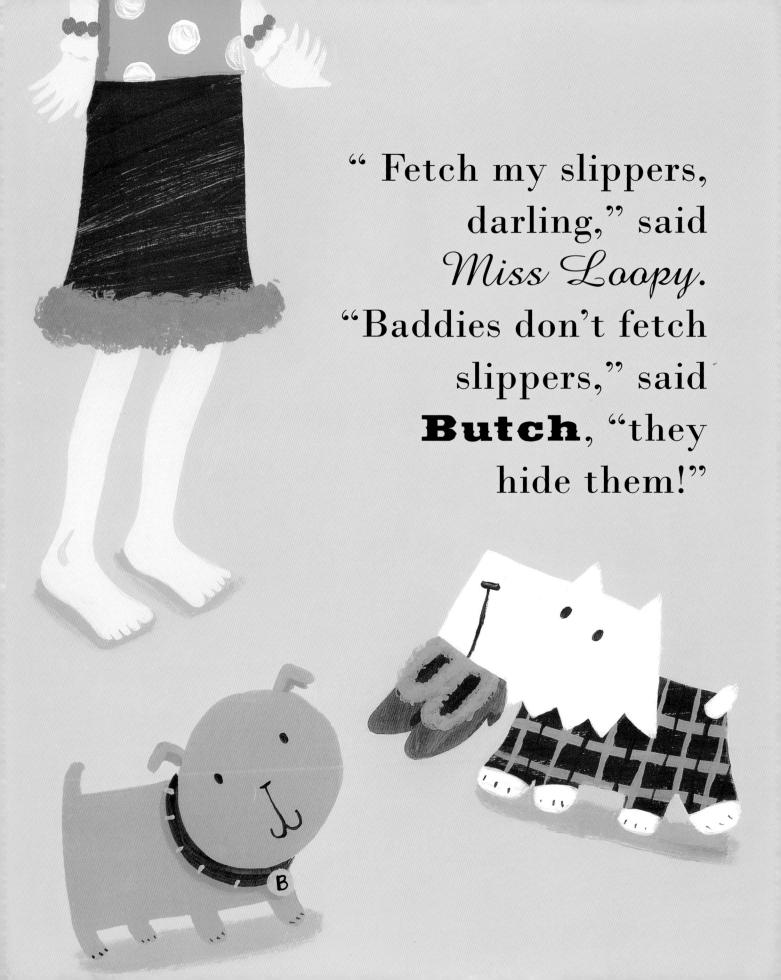

"Fetch my slippers, darling," said *Miss Loopy*. "Baddies don't fetch slippers," said **Butch**, "they hide them!"

"Good boy, coo-chi-coo!" said *Miss Loopy* and she tickled **Victor's** tummy.
"Baddies don't have their tummies tickled," said **Butch**, "they are too busy stealing sausages!"

"And another thing," said **Butch**, "Baddies aren't called **Victor**. They have names like Buster or Knuckles. You're a useless baddie!"

Victor felt very sad. He tried to think of a way to show **Butch** what a brilliant baddie he was.

Later that afternoon, when
Miss Loopy took them shopping,
Victor saw a sign that said:

"NO DOGS ALLOWED."
This gave **Victor** an idea . . .
and he told **Butch**.

"Watch this!" said **Victor**. "I'm going to run into that shop where it says "NO DOGS ALLOWED.""

Butch was very impressed.
Victor ran into the shop . . .

. . .then straight back out
again! He felt terrible for
being so naughty so he
shouted to the shopkeeper,
"Sorry about that!"
"Baddies don't say sorry,"
said **Butch** and he
laughed at **Victor** all
the way home.

But **Victor** didn't care because he didn't want to be a baddie now. "I wasn't cut out for a life of crime," he said.

Suddenly the door bell rang. *Miss Loopy* opened the door and there stood *Miss Froopy-Frou-Frou.* "Hello, *Miss Froopy-Frou-Frou,*" said *Miss Loopy.* "Come in."

"Where is my darling pup?"
cried *Miss Froopy-Frou-Frou*.
"Come to Mummikins,
my little poochie-poo.
Have you missed me?
Come on, poochie-poochie-
poochie-poo!"
And *Miss Froopy-Frou-Frou*
picked up **Butch** and
tickled his tummy.

Butch blushed.

"Baddies don't blush!" said **Victor**.

"Bye, bye," said *Miss Froopy-Frou-Frou.* "Bye, bye," called *Miss Loopy.*

"Bye, bye, Poochie-poochie-poochie-poo!" said **Victor**.